THIS BOOK BELONGS TO

For Fleur – LB
For Nicole and Jeffrey – RLO

Farshore

First published in Great Britain 2021 by Farshore
An imprint of HarperCollins*Publishers*
1 London Bridge Street, London SE1 9GF

farshore.co.uk

HarperCollins*Publishers*
1st Floor, Watermarque Building, Ringsend Road
Dublin 4, Ireland

Text copyright © Farshore 2021
Illustration copyright © David O'Connell 2021
The moral rights of the author and illustrator have been asserted.

ISBN 978 0 7555 0191 5
Printed in Great Britain by CPI Group
1

A CIP catalogue record for this title is available from the British Library.

MIX
Paper from
responsible sources
FSC™ C007454

THE NAUGHTIEST UNICORN

ON HOLIDAY

PIP BIRD

ILLUSTRATED BY DAVID O'CONNELL

Farshore

Contents

CHAPTER ONE
Wild Boars and Sleeping Bags

Mira Desai wriggled forward on the ground. She didn't have long to make the daring dash across the lava-filled forest floor and up to the tree-top castle.

She could hear the cries of the terrifying Wild Wood Boar behind her, getting closer and closer. The lava lapped at the edges of her protective body armour. Just a few centimetres more . . .

'MIRAAAA!' roared the GIANT boar, just as

Mira launched herself through the gates of the castle.

'YAAAAAAAAAAAAYY!' she yelled at the top of her voice and wriggled on the floor in celebration.

'Oh my gosh, I'm so sorry,' said Mira's mum to the other people on her video-conferencing call.

She turned around and looked at Mira on the floor. 'Mira, why are you in a sleeping bag?' she hissed crossly.

'It's MY sleeping bag!' yelled another voice, as the Wild Wood Boar, also known as Mira's big sister Rani, came crashing into the room. Rani started tugging at the sleeping bag. Mira burrowed deeper inside.

'I've got to practise for camping!' Mira said.

'You've got to look after my things or I will throw all of your stuff into a skip,' growled Rani.

Mira's mum rolled Mira out of the room. Rani slid along behind, still clinging on to the sleeping bag, as the door slammed shut behind them.

Then Rani tickled Mira until Mira wriggled so much that she slipped out of the sleeping bag. Rani grabbed it.

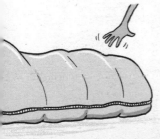

3

'The Unicorn School outdoor adventure holiday is *proper* camping. Your weird games won't help you,' said Rani, glaring at Mira and carefully rolling up the sleeping bag.

Mira hugged her knees with excitement. Rani was right. The Unicorn School outdoor adventure holiday wouldn't be like her games . . . it would be even better! Because going camping at Unicorn School meant unicorns would be there – and unicorns make everything approximately one hundred million times better.

Rani walked across the landing and put the sleeping bag neatly in the box of camping equipment that she had taken when she'd been on the Unicorn School outdoor adventure holiday. When Mum and Dad had said Rani had to give the camping equipment to Mira for her trip, Rani had grudgingly agreed – but not before she'd written 'RANI' everywhere in giant letters and made a list of everything so she could make sure that Mira brought it back.

'What is proper camping like, then?' said Mira, looking through the box and picking up a spoon.

Rani batted the spoon out of Mira's hand. 'Well, you walk out into the forest for a really long time, and then you put up the tent and sleep in it.'

Mira waited expectantly to hear more.

'And it's super dangerous and I had to wrestle a bear,' added Rani.

'COOL!' said Mira.

Rani started to tell her about all the other things they got up to on the holiday, while at the same time writing her name in GIANT letters on a tiny saucepan.

Nestled into the camping equipment box
was a packet of toffees. Mira felt
a happy glow looking at those.
Toffees made her think of her
unicorn, Dave.

Everyone at Unicorn School had
a Unicorn Best Friend Forever, and Dave was
Mira's. He wasn't like other unicorns. He was
more greedy than glittery, more interested in
doughnuts than rainbows, and he had a habit
of ruining magical moments by doing a giant
poo. But Mira had the most fun EVER with her
UBFF. When Mira had told Dave that they'd
be able to tell stories and eat sweets round a
campfire on their holiday, Dave had woken up

and done a fart of happiness that lasted seventeen seconds, which Mira thought must be some kind of world record.

'. . . but THE MOST exciting thing on the trip,' Rani was saying, 'is the Golden Marshmallow.'

Mira snapped out of her daydream and looked up from the camping box. 'The golden what now?' she asked.

'The Golden Marshmallow. It's super rare. There's only one, and no one has ever found it, but it's giant and golden,' said Rani. 'And it's said to be the tastiest toasted marshmallow that has ever been tasted or toasted in all of history.'

Mira gasped. That sounded amazing. Then she had a thought. 'If no one has ever found the

Golden Marshmallow, then how do you know it exists?' she said.

Rani looked smug. 'Well, me and my friends saw it when we were doing the ropes course, just for a second, glowing between some trees. So make sure you have these binoculars with you when you do the ropes course as it's *definitely* somewhere nearby.' She held up a pair of blue binoculars. 'But DON'T break them!' she said fiercely.

Then Rani closed the box and wrote on the top:

Mira felt the glowing feeling again. This was PERFECT! The thought of going camping with unicorns had made the holiday a hundred million times better, but going camping with unicorns AND having a secret quest to find a special golden treat made it a GATRILLION times better! (She was pretty sure that a gatrillion came after a hundred million.) She and Dave would find the Golden Marshmallow and then bring it back for everyone as an AMAZING surprise.

This really was going to be the best adventure EVER!

CHAPTER TWO
Just the Essentials

As Mira waited in the leisure centre car park by some bins (this was where the magical portal to Unicorn School was), she began to wonder if she might have brought a tiny bit too much stuff. Her rucksack was packed full and towered above her, making her feel ever so slightly off balance.

But then she saw Raheem, one of her best friends at Unicorn School. He was holding his little sister's hand and singing the Ten Rules of Safety song. Tia was too young to go to Unicorn School just yet, but she always came to wave off her big brother. Raheem's rucksack was as big as Mira's.

'I've brought two of everything — just in case,' he said. 'You can never be too prepared.'

Then Mira saw Darcy, her other best friend at Unicorn School. Darcy was wheeling towards Raheem and Tia, followed by her mum and dad,

who each had about six different bags and suitcases.

'Mira, hi!' Darcy did a spinning wheelie and held up her hand for a high five as Mira ran over.

"WE'RE GOING ON HOLIDAY!" Mira yelled.

She launched herself at her friends. Raheem quickly stepped behind Tia, who giggled and took Darcy's high five instead of Mira. Darcy's mum and dad each managed a small wave as they struggled under the weight of all Darcy's luggage.

'What did you bring?' asked Mira, staring.

'Outdoor clothes, summer clothes, fancy dress clothes,' said Darcy, counting them off on her fingers. 'Sleeping bag, inflatable bed, duvet, hot tub, torch, karaoke microphone – just the essentials really.'

Then Mira heard another voice. She saw

Jake climbing out of his parents' car. Jake was also her friend, though they often got annoyed with each other. Mira thought Jake was a bit of a know-it-all sometimes, and Jake would get cross when Dave misbehaved. He especially didn't like it when Dave farted near his unicorn, Pegasus, because Pegasus had a sensitive nose. Unfortunately Dave farted near Pegasus ALL the time.

'Jake will have brought LOADS of stuff,' Mira said to Darcy and Raheem, who both nodded in

agreement. Jake always had the latest everything, so he would definitely have all the coolest camping gear.

But as Jake arrived by the bins, they all stared. He didn't have any bags at all.

'What are you looking at?' he said, frowning.

'Jake, it's the Unicorn School outdoor adventure holiday!' said Mira.

'Yeah, I know,' said Jake. 'And?'

'And you've forgotten all of your stuff,' said Darcy.

Mira felt bad for Jake. He was a bit annoying, but she wouldn't want anyone to have to miss out on the coolest camping trip ever. Then she had a thought . . .

'It's okay,' she said in relief. 'Raheem's brought two of everything!'

Raheem beamed. 'I *said* you can never be too prepared!'

'Guys,' said Jake, holding up his hand. 'I've got everything I need.' He turned around.

Mira peered at Jake's back. He was wearing the tiniest rucksack she had ever seen.

'I've watched all of Adam Frog's *Wild Survival Skills*,' said Jake. 'Adam Frog says you don't need stuff to survive in the wild. You need SKILLS.' He tapped his finger on the side of his head. Then he strode off with his tiny bag towards the magic portal.

'I just don't know how he managed to fit a sleeping bag in there,' said Raheem.

'You couldn't even get a phone in there!' said Darcy, pulling out her own phone and taking a selfie with all her luggage.

It was time to go. Raheem gave Tia a goodbye hug, then slipped through the bushes. Mira helped Darcy's parents send her luggage through before her. Then Mira gripped her rucksack straps tightly and headed through the magic portal!

WHOOSH WHIZZ KAPOW!

Mira zoomed up and over the
magical rainbow of light. Her tummy
went all wibbly-wobbly as if she was on
a rollercoaster. This always happened, but today
Mira could feel her backpack going all wibbly-
wobbly too as the things she had stuffed in there
started to fall out. As she bumped down on to
the Landing Haystack, a hiking boot poked her
in the bottom. Then a tin mug fell on her head
and a pair of balled-up socks flew away
into the paddock, smacking Miss Hind
in the face.

'My bag!' Mira yelled, as she
slid off the Landing Haystack.

Mira's belongings were scattered all over the paddock. Flo had a pair of Mira's pants on her head and Raheem's unicorn Brave had her yellow raincoat hanging from his horn.

Darcy and Raheem and their unicorns, Star and Brave, helped Mira collect her things together and put them back in the rucksack. Mira was very relieved to see her special toy monkey, Ferdinand, sticking out of a haystack. She put him safely back in the pocket of her bag.

All around the paddock, children were reuniting with their unicorns. Raheem's unicorn, Brave, was wearing a head torch, knee pads and a waterproof poncho. And Mira didn't recognise Star at first, as she was wearing what looked like a giant sack with her horn poking out of the top.

'She's a walking tent,' said Darcy. 'I'm planning on stopping for brunch on the way.'

But where was Dave? Mira couldn't wait to see him and tell him about the Golden Marshmallow – he would be so excited. Mira had already decided not to tell anyone else about it, so that when she found the Golden Marshmallow it would be an epic surprise for the class!

Mira knew the best way to find her unicorn was with snacks. But as she pulled the toffees out of her bag, the packet ripped open, scattering sweets all around the paddock.

There was a sudden thundering of hooves.

Then there was a blur of white, zooming

closer. Mira grinned as the tiny unicorn-shaped

blur **WHIZZED** around the paddock, hoovering

up every single toffee. When he'd eaten them all,

Dave skidded to a halt next to Mira. He nuzzled her face and burped a toffee burp.

'He's a sweet vacuum cleaner!' said Seb, sounding impressed.

'I'm going to eat *all* my food like that from now on,' said Flo.

CHAPTER THREE
Special Treasure

The other classes started making their way down to the school for assembly but Class Red and their unicorns waited in the paddock. As soon as their teacher, Miss Glitterhorn, arrived they would be going to straight to the Wild Woods to start their outdoor adventure holiday!

They started to put their bags on to their unicorns' backs. Mira soon gave up as Dave shook himself like a wet dog every time she tried, so her bag kept falling off. Everyone had to carry one of Darcy's bags as well, because she'd brought so many.

'What *is* all of this?' said Jake disapprovingly, as he picked up one from the mountain of bags.

'Just my holiday essentials,' Darcy said again with a shrug. 'Hey – be careful with my bookcase.'

Jake folded his arms. 'Well, I have packed only the *real* essentials. Adam Frog says a true survivalist needs nothing but their wits and mother nature. And a small penknife.'

'I'll take that, thank you, Jake.' Miss Glitterhorn confiscated the penknife and ticked the children off the list on her clipboard. 'Right. Now I need a volunteer to carry something very special for everyone.'

She pointed at a wooden box with a big padlock on it. It looked a bit like a treasure chest. All the hands and hooves went up in the air, except for Dave, who was having a sneaky nap.

'In this box,' said Miss Glitterhorn, 'we have the marshmallows for the special Unicorn School campfire that we'll have on the last night of the holiday.'

At the mention of marshmallows Dave immediately woke up and trotted up to Miss Glitterhorn with his hoof in the air.

'We've taken some extra precautions this year to secure the box,' said Miss Glitterhorn. She narrowed her eyes at Dave, who was hopping around, snorting and waving his hoof right in front of her, desperate to be picked. 'Just in case one of the unicorns gets a bit peckish before the campfire.'

Much to Dave's disappointment, Miss Glitterhorn chose Raheem and Brave to carry the special marshmallow box as a reward for being so well prepared for the trip. 'Line up with your unicorns, Class Red,' she said. 'It's time for your outdoor adventure holiday!'

Class Red cheered and Dave did a huge happy poo.

∪∪∪

The sun was beating down on Class Red as they trekked to the Wild Woods. Mira took a sip of

water. Her throat was dry and she wiped her sweaty forehead with the back of her sleeve.

'Are we nearly there yet?' Tamsin asked Miss Glitterhorn.

'Miss Glitterhorn, Dave can't go on!' Mira called to the teacher.

'Mira, we haven't even left the Grand Paddock. Everybody, pull yourselves together,' Miss Glitterhorn said with a frown.

Dave was having one of the grumpy naps he had when he was hungry and Mira couldn't move him. So Miss Glitterhorn agreed that they could all have a 'very brief' snack break. Dave immediately woke up and trotted over to the locked marshmallow box. He sniffed all around the box and scrabbled at the lock with his hooves, but it was no use. There was no way in.

'Dave!' shouted Miss Glitterhorn, spotting him.

Dave scurried back over to Mira and burrowed his head into her bag to hide (and find something to eat).

'Snack break over!' said Miss Glitterhorn and they all started walking again. Mira gave Dave a banana to give him some energy.

'I heard you get so hungry in the woods you have to peel bark off trees with your teeth and chew it,' said Tamsin.

'I heard wild boars are waiting to eat your breakfast,' said Seb.

'Not boars, bears,' said Mira. 'My sister said she had to wrestle one.'

'Well, I heard there are crocodiles in the river and you have to fight them to get to the toilet block,' said Jake.

Raheem stopped suddenly. 'But there is an actual toilet block, right?'

His unicorn Brave shivered.

'I'm not taking any chances,' said Darcy. 'I've brought my own portaloo.'

Jake tutted. 'Adam Frog would never bring a portaloo with him.'

'How does he go to the loo, then?' said Freya.

'He buries it,' said Jake.

Everyone stared at him. Then lots of them asked Darcy if she needed any more help with her bags and especially if she needed a hand carrying the portaloo.

'That reminds me,' said Raheem. 'We have to bury the unicorns' poo. It attracts animals. I've brought some spare poo shovels.'

Mira grinned to herself. With Dave as her UBFF she carried a poo shovel with her ALL the time. Most unicorn poos were neat and glittery, but Dave's were giant. He liked to do them in inconvenient places too, like in the middle of a corridor or right by the table in the lunch hall.

'Hey Dave,' she whispered, giving him a scratch behind the ears. She'd been waiting to tell him the extra reason to be excited about this trip! 'My sister told me that in the Wild Woods there's a Golden Marshmallow! It's the tastiest toasted marshmallow that has ever been tasted or toasted in the whole of history! We have to find it!'

Dave stopped so suddenly that Mira fell off his back. He looked at her, his eyes wide. Then he farted a cloud of pink bubbles.

All the other unicorns stopped too and watched as another stream of pink bubbles shot

out of Dave's bum and floated into the air.
Pegasus and Jake, who had been behind Dave,
shielded their faces.

'He's a toffee vacuum cleaner AND he has a
magical bum!' said Seb.

'Dave?' said Mira. Her UBFF was now

foaming at the mouth with pink sparkly glitter foam. 'Did you eat the cupcake shower gel that was in my bag?'

Dave nodded and spat out the glittery shower-gel lid. Mira gave him a drink from her water bottle. Dave nuzzled her face, which is a unicorn version of a hug.

Mira grinned at her unicorn.'I can't wait to find the Golden Marshmallow!' she whispered. Having a secret plan with your UBFF was the BEST!

CHAPTER FOUR
Into the Wild Woods

Very soon Class Red reached the entrance to the Wild Woods. It was covered in sparkle spider webs, and as soon as Brave spotted them he yelped and cantered off. Sparkle spiders were the one thing that this very brave unicorn was scared of.

Just as Raheem was leading Brave back to the woods with a safety scarf around his eyes, Class Red heard a swooshing. Then they heard a swishing. Then they heard a –

`AAAA-AAAAAAAAAAAAAAA!`

Leaves and twigs fell as something clattered towards them, swinging on vines through the treetops. It came closer. The children whispered nervously to each other. Was it an orangutan? Was it a bear?

'It's a tree alien,' said Flo confidently.

Dave shook Mira off his back and then leaped into her arms.

With a final **'AAAAAA!'** a short, wiry woman with a shock of wild grey hair flung herself from a tree vine and landed in front of Class Red. Mira noticed that she wasn't wearing any shoes.

'Welcome to the Wild Woods,' the woman shouted. 'Enter if you dare!'

Miss Glitterhorn took a step back and cleared her throat. 'Class Red, please give a warm hello to Ms Mustang.'

'Gooood moooorniiiinng Miizzzzz Mustang,' said Class Red.

A green unicorn camouflaged with mud came crawling out of the woods behind her. Ms Mustang introduced him as her unicorn, Wildebeest. 'Well, it's time for me to be getting back to school,' said Miss Glitterhorn. 'I'll miss you so much, Class Red! The comfortable bed, nice hot shower and peace and quiet might make up for it though. Have a super holiday! See you in two days!'

She jumped on her unicorn, Heathcliff, and cantered quickly back in the direction of school.

Ms Mustang grinned at Class Red and shook some leaves from her hair.

Darcy's hand shot up. 'Do you actually live in the woods?'

'Are there really bears?' asked Raheem.

'Do you enjoy being a tree alien?' asked Flo.

'Do we have to bury our poo?' said Tamsin.

Ms Mustang flung her head back and laughed.

Mira thought she looked a bit like an old, muddy Peter Pan.

'All in good time, young friends! Follow me!'

Ms Mustang skipped off into the Wild Woods. Class Red looked at each other and then followed her as quickly as they could, crashing through the undergrowth and banging into each other. Wildebeest disappeared silently into a holly bush.

'Well Class Red, you're lucky that you weren't here yesterday as there was a HUGE storm in the woods. The wind blew the roof off my treehouse!' said Ms Mustang, as she skipped ahead. 'It's still a bit windy today, but the storm has passed.'

'Wow, you actually live in a treehouse?' asked Seb, struggling to keep up.

'Only when it's too wet to sleep under the stars,' replied Ms Mustang.

'Coooool,' said Jake.

'Where do you poo in a treehouse?' asked Freya.

Ms Mustang winked at Flo. 'An excellent question! I've whittled a plumbing system out of reeds. And speaking of poo,' she continued, 'we have to be bear-safe in the Wild Woods. So always lock your snack boxes and string them up high in a tree. And always, ALWAYS bury your unicorns' poo.'

As Class Red followed Ms Mustang deeper

into the trees it became darker and damper. Everything smelled green, like grass just after the rain. They heard a gentle cooing from the treetops and snuffling from bushes along the path. The wind moved the branches of the trees around so they made a mysterious rustling sound. Mira breathed in the fresh, woodland air. She was so excited for the holiday to start – and for her secret Golden Marshmallow mission to begin! Even Dave seemed excited about everything, although Mira thought he might be sleepwalking and dreaming about food as his eyes were closed and he kept licking his lips.

A few minutes later Ms Mustang stopped at a clearing. She sniffed the air. 'This is the perfect place to set up your tents!' she said.

Wildebeest came bursting out of the bushes. He darted around the forest clearing and shimmied up a tree.

'Wow!' said Jake. 'Wildebeest is like the coolest unicorn ever!'

Mira saw Pegasus look down at his hooves sadly.

Ms Mustang divided Class Red into groups of three children, plus their unicorns, and gave each group a tent bag and patch of land. Mira and Dave

were put in a group with Jake and Pegasus and Raheem and Brave.

'Do we get a medal for the best tent?' asked Mira hopefully.

In all their lessons at Unicorn School they could get medals for doing things well. Despite Dave often getting into trouble, they had won a few medals, and Mira was always hopeful about getting more. Rani had *lots* of medals.

'No, survival is its own reward,' said Ms Mustang. 'But I *do* reward a job well done. Nature has more beautiful gifts to offer than any trophy. For example, Tamsin, I notice how neatly your rucksack is packed. Here is a precious feather from a peacock. Seb, well done cleaning up your unicorn's poo. Here is an unusual stone I found on the riverbed.'

Seb and Tamsin beamed as they went to collect their prizes.

Mira stuck up her hand. 'Can we convert pebbles and feathers and stuff into medals when we get back to Unicorn School?'

Ms Mustang ignored Mira and looked at the position of the sun. 'You have one hour to set up your tents and then you may open your snack boxes for lunch. First patrol to finish wins these special shells. What are you all waiting for? Go!'

'Right,' said Mira. 'Let's do this!'

Raheem took out the tent instructions and carefully unfolded them.

'Can I see those?' said Jake.

Raheem handed them over. Jake ripped the instructions in two.

'JAKE!' cried Mira and Raheem, and Brave gave an outraged snort.

'How are we going to put our tent up now?' said Mira.

'We don't need instructions. We just need our MINDS!' said Jake, tapping his head again.

'And instructions,' said Raheem. He carefully taped the instructions together using his Emergency Stationery kit.

'Whatever,' said Jake. 'You use your instructions. Pegasus and I will make our own tent out of twigs and mud.'

He stomped off across the clearing. Pegasus hesitated, looking a bit surprised, before trotting after him.

CHAPTER FIVE
Bad Leaves and Twig Tents

Mira and Raheem read the instructions carefully and began to put the tent up. Apart from a brief delay when Dave curled up in the ground sheet to have a nap and they had to tip him out, it was going quite well – mainly because Raheem had practised putting up a tent nineteen times in his garden before the trip. Mira looked around the campsite. Flo and Freya's tent was upside down, and Darcy and Star had got distracted making a video.

We might win! Mira thought.

Ms Mustang and Wildebeest were rolling logs into the middle of the clearing to make an eating area. 'Excellent work, everyone!' said the teacher. 'I shall just check on the special marshmallow box.'

Dave's ears pricked up and his nostrils went wide.

Oh no, thought Mira.

Dave galloped towards the snack box, but his hooves got tangled in Mira and Raheem's tent ropes. The ropes strained as Dave kept running. He reached the snack box and grabbed it with his hooves.

But then a sudden gust of wind made the tent

break free from its pegs and fly up into the air.
Mira, Raheem and Brave reached for it, but the
tent floated higher like a hot air balloon – taking
Dave with it!

The little unicorn gave a panicked whinny and
gripped the snack box tighter. The box started
to lift off the ground too. But as the tent rose
higher and pulled Dave upwards, the wooden
box slid out of his hooves and bounced on the
ground.

'NEEEEIIIIIIIIIGGGGGGGGGH!' howled
Dave.

'Dave!' yelled Mira, as her UBFF flew up into
the air.

Another strong gust of wind blew the tent,

but this time it went sideways and hit a tree.
The tent caught in the branches and Dave
dangled there, his bum sticking straight up in
the air.

'Who is disrespecting the trees?' said Ms
Mustang.

'It's Dave,' said Mira. 'But he didn't mean to
disrespect the trees. He was just a bit hungry and
wanted to have a look at the snack box.'

Dave neighed sadly again. Mira smiled at Ms
Mustang, hoping they wouldn't get told off.

Ms Mustang looked stern. 'You must NOT open
the special snack box until the night of the campfire.
Anyone who does will be in BIG trouble.'

Mira nodded. 'Dave definitely won't do that.'

Jake scoffed. 'He definitely will – *and* he'll eat all our marshmallows.'

There were some murmurs of agreement from the rest of the class.

Mira glared at her friends. They did have a point, but she didn't like people saying mean things about her UBFF!

'That is not the problem,' said Ms Mustang. 'I have plenty of my homemade nettle marshmallows you can eat.'

Class Red looked horrified.

'We must not open the snack box early, because bears love sweet treats most of all,' said Ms Mustang. 'And they have an excellent sense of smell.'

'He won't open it *and* he'll be super well behaved from now on, won't you, Dave?' called Mira.

Dave was wriggling his little legs in the air, trying to turn himself the right way round. He farted loudly.

'That means yes!' said Mira.

'Right, I need a nimble unicorn volunteer to climb up there and get him down,' said Ms Mustang. 'It won't be easy. He's very tangled.'

'I bet Wildebeest can do it,' said Jake.

Pegasus came speeding forward from behind Jake and took a daring leap at the tree. He collided with the trunk and slid slowly down to the ground.

Wildebeest darted out from a bush, jumped over Pegasus and shimmied up the tree. With a flick of his horn Wildebeest cut through the tent ropes and Dave fell down, landing on Pegasus with a thump. Then Wildebeest untangled the tent from the branches, grabbed hold of the ropes with his teeth and leaped down, using the

tent as a parachute. As he landed, he forward-
rolled and threw the tent to Raheem, who
caught it, his eyes wide with surprise.

The whole class clapped.

'I wish I'd filmed that!' said Jake.

Pegasus came walking over with Dave still

on his back. Dave was now quietly snoozing.
Pegasus blinked, still looking quite dazed from
colliding with the tree trunk.

Ms Mustang sighed and gave the special shells
to Flo, Seb and Tamsin for having their tent up
first and also for not putting it up a tree.

Mira breathed a sigh of relief. Dave was okay, and they hadn't got into too much trouble. If Ms Mustang didn't believe in giving medals, then she wouldn't believe in Havoc points either. Havoc points were what you got at Unicorn School if you were naughty, and if you got three then you got a detention.

Ms Mustang handed Mira a small brown leaf.

'Did I get a reward?' said Mira. This was better than she thought!

Ms Mustang shook her head. 'This is a Bad Leaf,' she said. 'You're getting this because your unicorn tried to get into the snack box *and* put your tent in a tree. If your team gets three Bad Leaves, you must sit out of the activities.'

'That's not fair!' said Jake. 'I had nothing to do with that tent. I was making my own.' He gestured at the pile of twigs next to him. 'It's not finished yet,' he added.

Ms Mustang peered at the twigs. 'That is two Bad Leaves for your team,' she said, handing another tiny leaf to Jake.

'What?!' said Jake, stunned. 'But that's not –'

Ms Mustang held up her hand. 'Teamwork is key to survival, and teams must work together at all times.'

Mira and Jake looked at each other. Their team would have to be on their best behaviour now, or they might miss out on the fun activities! Things were not going well . . .

CHAPTER SIX
Sink or Swim!

'Time for lunch!' called Ms Mustang a few minutes later.

Dave, who had been snoring away on Pegasus's back, immediately leaped off and trotted over to the log seating area. Mira followed him.

'Remember Dave, keep an eye open for any mysterious glowing lights in the woods,' she whispered to her unicorn. 'It might be the Golden Marshmallow!'

Dave nodded and peered into the woods,

although he did seem more interested in the
sandwiches and crisps.

Mira so hoped that she could find the Golden
Marshmallow and share it with the class. She felt
a shiver of excitement run up her spine as she
thought of all her friends sitting around the fire
and toasting a magical marshmallow . . .

'Anybody want a cookie?' called Darcy,
interrupting Mira's daydream.

'Yes please!' Mira turned around and saw
Darcy's tent. 'Whoa! Your tent is AWESOME!'

Darcy grinned and passed the giant plate of
cookies to Mira.

Freya and her unicorn, Princess, were in
Darcy's tent team and were sitting outside the

tent on deckchairs. Star tapped Darcy on the shoulder with her hoof and handed her an eye mask and a bathrobe.

'Ooh, spa time,' said Darcy. 'See you later.'

∪∪∪

After lunch, Class Red made sure that the tents were all zipped up and food was safely locked away. Then they walked down to the lake to start their first activity: raft-making.

As they trotted along the forest path, Mira looked around her. Ms Mustang was telling them that all kinds of different wildlife lived in the Wild Woods, from foxes and badgers to beavers and even snakes, which made some of

Class Red a bit nervous until Ms Mustang said they weren't poisonous ones.

But there was one thing Mira *really* wanted to see more of . . . the Golden Marshmallow! Getting the Bad Leaves had made Mira even more determined to find the yummy treasure. As they went further into the Wild Wood, she scanned the trees and the bushes for any glimpses of gold. She wished that she had remembered to bring Rani's binoculars with her.

Soon they could hear the splashing of running water. The path led out from the trees to the

bank of a small lake, with streams flowing into little waterfalls around the edge. The whole class whooped with excitement. They couldn't wait to build their very own raft!

Ms Mustang told them to gather in their teams and handed out orange lifejackets for them all to put on. Then she explained that they had to build a raft that would take them across the lake. The first team across would win.

Because Darcy and Freya only had each other (and their unicorns) in their team, Ms Mustang said they could have Wildebeest to help them.

Mira turned to Jake and Raheem. 'Right, team! So how do we build a raft?'

Jake folded his arms. 'In Adam Frog's *Wild Survival Skills* he made a raft out of some lily pads and he tied them together using weeds and spit. Let's do that.'

'Or I thought maybe we could hitch a ride across on a giant turtle?' said Mira. Ms Mustang hadn't said the raft *couldn't* be a turtle.

'Or we could use that stuff?' said Raheem, pointing at the edge of the lake where there were barrels, planks of wood, coils of roil and a sign that said:

Raft Materials

Jake shook his head. 'That's too easy. You wouldn't have ropes and barrels and planks in a real survival situation.'

'But this isn't a real survival situation, it's a challenge!' said Mira crossly.

Jake started to argue back, but then Raheem suggested they use Jake's materials AND the proper raft materials, and Ms Mustang popped up and gave him a shiny conker for good teamwork.

Mira, Dave, Raheem and Brave went to get barrels, planks and rope while Jake and Pegasus went to get lily pads and weeds. Mira looked around at the other teams. Flo's team had only got as far as laying out all their material on the

67

ground and Flo seemed to have tied a barrel to her leg. But Darcy and Freya were splashing about in the shallow water, having a chat, while Wildebeest made a very impressive-looking raft at lightning speed. Mira realised her team was going to have to be very quick to beat them!

Mira's team gathered all the materials together and got to work. Raheem showed the others the knots he'd learned to tie the barrels to the planks. Dave chewed the weeds to provide the spit and he only ate around half of them. Mira gave him a big hug. Jake covered the top of the raft with lily pads. Then Mira and Raheem went to find some sticks to use for oars while Jake made some last adjustments. Now their raft was ready!

They carried it down to the edge of the lake.
Flo's team were still tangled up in their ropes, but
Freya and Darcy were already setting off. Their
raft looked very secure and Darcy had added a
parasol on the back. She and Freya were sitting
on deckchairs either side of a blue cool box, while
Wildebeest sat at the front, holding a wooden oar
he'd just finished whittling with his teeth.

'Quick!' said Mira.

They put their raft into the water. It floated!
The children and their unicorns climbed aboard.
Brave pushed them off from the bank and they
sailed forward.

The raft immediately fell apart beneath them.
Mira, Raheem and Jake ended up on a barrel

each, while the wooden planks sank. The
unicorns slid into the water. Mira could see
the lake wasn't deep at all, because the unicorns
were standing up. Dave, who had much shorter
legs than the other unicorns, held on to Mira's
barrel.

'But I did my special knots!' said Raheem,
looking around in disbelief.

'I, um, swapped the ropes for some plaited grass,'
said Jake. 'It usually makes really strong rope.'

Mira sighed. 'Well, at least we're not last.'

But just as she said that, Flo, Tamsin, Seb and their unicorns came floating slowly past on the back of a giant turtle.

Flo waved at them. 'He's called Basil!' she yelled.

Now they *were* last. And away in the distance, Darcy and Freya were already nearly at the other side of the lake.

CHAPTER SEVEN
Fart Jets

Raheem got his telescope out of his emergency bumbag and squinted into it. 'Darcy's got ice lollies!' he said.

Next to Mira, Dave flipped around on to his front. His ears pricked up and his eyes went wide. Mira heard a strange rumbling sound. Her UBFF shot forward in the water, pushing Mira's barrel in front of him. A stream of bubbles sprayed out from his bum.

Mira had a brilliant idea.

'Quick, all hold hands!' she said.

Jake looked unsure, but then Dave did another powerful underwater fart and Mira's barrel shot forward again. Raheem and Jake paddled over, so that the three barrels lined up, with Mira's in the middle. Then they linked arms. Brave and Pegasus swam behind the barrels, either side of Dave.

'GO DAVE! GO GET THOSE ICE LOLLIES!' yelled Mira.

Dave let off the strongest fart jet yet. Bubbles streamed out behind them and they rocketed through the water. They zoomed past Flo's team on Basil the turtle. They were gaining on Darcy and Freya. They were going faster and faster, all thanks to the power of Dave's bum. Mira felt very proud.

They were soon right behind Darcy and Freya's raft. Wildebeest narrowed his eyes and starting rowing faster, until his oar was a blur.

Dave was looking a bit tired.

'We're slowing down!' said Jake.

'I think he's running low on fart!' said Mira.

Raheem looked in his telescope again. 'She hasn't just got ice lollies. There are CHOC ICES!'

Dave neighed. There was a rumble and then the most powerful jet of bubbles yet shot out of his bottom.

'Hold on tight!' yelled Mira.

They raced through the water, past Darcy's boat – Dave grabbing a choc ice as they did – and came to a stop on the riverbank.

'You are the winners!' announced Ms Mustang with a big grin, and she handed them some strands of pond weed.

∪∪∪

Soggy but happy and munching on choc ices and lollies, Class Red and their unicorns walked back along the forest path to the campsite.

Mira was at the back as usual on Dave, but she didn't mind going slowly. She was peering through the branches for any glimpses of gold. When they got back to the campsite the sun was setting. The sky was a dusky blue and the tents were casting shadows across the clearing. It was also a little chillier than when they'd left, so Mira went to get her hoodie from the tent. When she came out, she saw Wildebeest had gathered branches into a pile next to the logs they'd sat on at lunch. Then he started the campfire by rubbing a stick on his horn. Soon the fire was crackling away.

'Ooooh!' said Class Red in unison.

'So. Cool,' said Jake, and Pegasus sniffed.

'Is it time for toasted marshmallows?' said Seb hopefully.

'No,' said Ms Mustang. 'We'll have those at our special campfire party tomorrow night.'

She tapped the locked marshmallow box. Everyone immediately looked at Dave, who was snoozing on a log.

'Tonight I am making you a traditional forest dinner,' Ms Mustang continued.

'Oh, can't we forage for food?' said Jake. 'That's what Adam Frog does.'

'I saw these people living in the woods who

had to eat insects and kangaroo bums,' said Flo.

'What, on TV?' said Tamsin, horrified.

'Can't remember,' said Flo.

'That is a wonderful idea,' said Ms Mustang. Tamsin shrieked. 'Not the bums, the foraging,' the teacher continued. 'While I get things ready, you can all forage for a tasty snack. But just around the campsite area, as it is getting dark. And DON'T eat anything without showing me first.'

Wildebeest crawled forward to the edge of the clearing, sniffing the air. Jake tied a bandana round his head and copied him.

Mira and Dave found a spot round the other side of their tent. If there was one thing Dave was good

at, it was foraging for snacks! He soon sniffed out a clump of truffle mushrooms. Unfortunately, every time Mira went to dig one up, Dave ate it. In the end, she only managed to dig up one truffle, which was very tiny and shrivelled.

'Don't worry,' said Raheem, walking over with Brave. 'You could just say it's a canape. My mum serves them when her friends come over.'

'What's a canape?' said Mira.

'It's like food, but really, really small,' said Raheem.

'What did you find?' said Mira, holding her canape in the air as Dave made a lunge for it.

'Blackberries served on a piece of bark,' said Raheem.

Most people had found berries like Raheem, though Flo had moulded a handful of grass into the shape of a chicken leg. Jake had made 'leaf crisps'. But they were mostly looking forward to eating food they hadn't found on the ground. Mira wondered what they would be eating. When Rani had gone camping, they'd eaten baked potatoes with beans!

When they got back to the campfire, Ms Mustang was lowering a steaming vat of something from her tree house. 'Your special forest dinner,' she said. 'Nettle soup with nettle bread surprise!'

They stared at her.

'What's the surprise?' said Freya.

'Nettle butter!' said Ms Mustang.

'Um, Ms Mustang?' said Tamsin. 'What's for pudding?'

'Mud pie,' said Ms Mustang. 'Made with real mud!'

There was a horrified silence.

'Do you have any more cookies, Darcy?' whispered Tamsin.

But then Ms Mustang burst out laughing. 'I'm just joking with you! It's nettle trifle.'

When they finished dinner, it was properly dark. Through the branches above their heads Mira could see the stars twinkling against the

inky black sky. After the nettle trifle (which was actually okay, just very green) they'd sung songs around the campfire, led by Darcy and Star. Though they'd had to put their hands over their ears when all the unicorns sang the Unicorn National Anthem, as unicorn singing is very loud and very screechy.

Now the campfire was just red glowing embers. Mira yawned. It was time for their first night in the Wild Woods! Ms Mustang told them to make their way towards their tents and get ready for bed.

Dave was having one of his after-dinner sleeps, curled up in a ball on the log next to Mira. She gave him a little nudge. He woke up, rolled off the log and did a surprise poo on the ground. Mira whipped out her poo shovel.

'It's the ropes course tomorrow, Dave,' Mira whispered excitedly as she cleaned up the poo. 'That's where Rani thought she spotted the Golden Marshmallow! I'm going to try my best to spot it and I won't forget to take Rani's binoculars with me this time.'

Dave did a whisper-whinny and licked her face.

'But you know what that means, don't you?' Mira reminded him. 'No more trying to get into the locked marshmallow box. Otherwise we'll get another Bad Leaf and we'll miss our chance to find the magical treat.'

Dave rolled his eyes but also nuzzled Mira's

arm, which she knew meant 'yes'.

Mira switched on her torch and they made their way towards the tent. Raheem was already inside, organising his socks, Pegasus and Brave were playing cards and Jake was going around the outside 'making the tent bear-safe'.

Mira snuggled down into her sleeping bag. She heard an owl hoot up in the trees. This was such an adventure!

CHAPTER EIGHT
Tent Party!

Jake got into the tent and started doing up all the zips on the door. 'Right,' he said when he'd finished. 'Now no one can get in or out.'

'What if we need the loo?' said Raheem.

'Well, yeah,' said Jake, 'we can get out, if we have to, but no one can get in. That's the point.'

'What are we doing now?' said Darcy from next to Mira, making them all jump.

'Why aren't you in your giant tent?' asked Jake, shining his torch over at Darcy.

Darcy shrugged. 'It's a bit quiet.'

From behind Brave, Star snorted in agreement.

'We're supposed to be in our own tents,' said Jake.

'We thought it would be fun to be together,' said Freya from next to Raheem.

'I came in because I was getting a bit freaked out by the forest noises,' said Tamsin by the door.

'How did you all get in here?' said Jake. 'This is supposed to be about survival, not a tent party!'

There was a zzzzzzzip sound and Flo and Seb and their unicorns crawled through the door of the tent. 'We've come to join the tent party!' said Seb.

'Yay!' said everyone but Jake. Pegasus was clapping his hooves but then Jake looked at him and he stopped.

Jake sighed and shook his head. 'This would never have happened if you'd let me build my tent of leaves like I wanted.'

Suddenly there was a scrabbling and scratching sound outside.

'No one else is coming in!' said Jake, zipping up the door again.

'But Jake,' said Mira, shining her torch around the tent. 'We're all here.'

They all looked at the door of the tent.

'Maybe it's Ms Mustang?' said Tamsin, backing away.

'No, she's in her tree house,' said Freya.

They listened. Sure enough they could hear Ms Mustang, up in the trees, doing her late-night yodelling.

There was another weird scratching noise from outside the tent.

'Perhaps it's Wildebeest?' said Jake.

'I saw him when I went to brush my teeth,' said Seb. 'He sleeps upside down on a rope, dangling from the tree house like a bat.'

'It's probably one of those child–eating badgers,' said Flo. 'Let's have a look.'

She turned round and unzipped the door. Everyone inside the tent gasped. Flo shone her torch around in the darkness. Mira gulped and peered forward to see. There was nothing there.

'See? I said it was nothing to worry about,' said Jake, zipping up the tent again. He looked nervously at the door.

'Can we stay here?' said Tamsin.

'You can stay for a little bit,' Jake said.

Some of them had brought their sleeping bags and Raheem had spares for the others. Tamsin, Seb and Freya had brought cuddly toys too. Mira was pleased about that. She had brought her cuddly monkey, Ferdinand, but she wasn't sure if she would be the only one. She'd had Ferdinand since she was little. Over the years he'd lost most of his fur and one eye, and Rani said he stank. But Mira loved how he smelled like home.

Inside the tent, everyone snuggled down inside their sleeping bags. Mira grinned to herself. It was fun having a tent party! Plus the forest noises were a *bit* scary, so it was nice having all her friends there. Even though every time there was a new sound they all froze, except for Flo, who was excited about seeing the child–eating badgers.

'What's *that*?' said Jake.

He pointed up at the top of the tent. They all screamed. Mira threw her hands over her face. Dave scrambled into Mira's sleeping bag and huddled in a ball at the bottom. Mira slowly opened one eye and looked to where Jake was pointing.

'I think it's the branches outside, casting a shadow on the tent,' said Raheem.

'Yeah, I know,' said Jake, still staring up at the weird shape. 'I was just testing you.'

'Well, can you not?' said Tamsin. 'I thought there was a child-eating badger up there.'

Flo laughed. 'Don't worry – they can't fly. They just eat people.'

Mira twizzled the top of her torch, making the light blink. The shadow on the tent roof had given her an idea. 'We should play shadow puppets!' she said.

Everyone agreed that would be really fun and Jake didn't seem to be as keen as before to make them all leave.

'Rabbit!' said Seb, holding his hand in front of his torch and casting a rabbit-shaped shadow on the wall.

'Rabbiticorn!' said Darcy, leaning over and giving the rabbit a horn.

'Awkward Turtle!' said Mira, putting one hand over the other to be the shell and then using her thumbs for the turtle's swimming legs. It was one her sister had shown her. They all laughed as the Awkward Turtle swam slowly along the wall of the tent. And then they did all the animals they could think of – bat, reindeer, elephant – with Darcy adding horns to all of them.

'Okay, okay,' said Jake. 'Get ready, cos this one's going to be the best one ever.'

Pegasus held the torch and Jake positioned his hands.

A huge shadow rose up on the side of the tent. It wasn't like any animal that Mira had ever seen before. It had a huge head and a weird tail, with fur and claws. The shadow opened its mouth to reveal two giant fangs.

'Wow, Jake,' said Freya. 'That's so good!'

'Very real,' said Darcy.

It did look really realistic, Mira thought.
She glanced over at Jake. He was staring at
the shadow too. And his arms were folded.

Then the shadow creature let out a long
low growl.

Everyone screamed and the unicorns screeched.

'Okay, shadow puppet game is over!' said
Tamsin, grabbing the torch from Pegasus and
switching it off.

They all agreed that it was probably time
to get some sleep and everyone snuggled up
together. Mira tried not to think about what
had made the scary shadow. She was pretty

sure it hadn't been Jake . . .

Something tapped Mira on the shoulder, making her jump. She turned round to see Dave's little hoof poking out of her sleeping bag. Mira breathed out, relieved. 'What is it, Dave?'

The little unicorn wriggled out of the sleeping bag and pointed outside. Mira frowned, confused. What did he want? But then she saw his tail rising up in the air.

Oh no.

'Dave needs the loo,' she said. 'I'm going to have to take him to the toilet bucket.' Ms Mustang had been *very* firm about unicorns only using the toilet bucket when they were in the campsite.

'Can't he go on his own?' said Jake.

Dave shook his head and whinnied indignantly.

'No, I think he's scared,' said Mira.

Jake rolled his eyes. 'Okay, well be quick!' he said, starting to unzip the tent.

Mira pulled her hoodie back on over her pyjamas, put her trainers on and picked up her torch. But the thought of leaving the tent was making her heart thump a little bit harder. She was feeling a bit scared too . . .

'Maybe you and Pegasus could come with us, Jake?' she said, as she and Dave climbed out of the tent.

'No thanks. Bye!' said Jake, zipping up the door behind them.

A light breeze blew through the campsite,

making some of the tent ropes flap. Up in the trees, an owl hooted. Mira took a deep breath and walked in the direction of the toilet bucket.

She was sure she could hear that scrabbling sound again, in the bushes. She kept seeing things move out of the corner of her eye too – but when she looked round, everything was still and silent.

When they got to the toilet area, Dave trotted off towards the unicorns' toilet buckets and Mira waited outside. When he'd finished, they ran quickly back to the tent. Mira snuggled back down inside her sleeping bag, relieved to see just the shadows of branches on the tent roof – and no shadow creatures!

CHAPTER NINE
Marshmallow Mystery

The early morning sun shone on the campsite.
Mira stepped outside the tent and smiled. It was
so special to wake up on holiday in the middle
of a forest! It was hard to believe it had seemed a
scary place last night, now that there was nothing
but the sound of birdsong and bickering in the air.

'You're doing it all wrong,' said Jake.

Flo yawned. 'You're supposed to toast your
breakfast on a camping holiday.'

Jake tutted. 'Yeah, but you're toasting cereal.

I'm toasting toast. From bark bread. Which I made of bark. That's proper camping holiday breakfast toast.'

'Don't tell anyone, but we've got Pop-Tarts,' whispered Darcy as she went round the campsite. 'Star's cooking them to order in our yurt. Want to put your name down?'

Mira got her sneaky Pop-Tart and went over to where Wildebeest was running an early-morning activity, showing the unicorns how to tie different knots in rope. Flo had finished her toasted cereal and started plaiting all the unicorns' manes. She said it was like knots but prettier. Tamsin was sizzling some sausages on the campfire.

Ms Mustang strode over, looking stern and sweaty. 'I have just come back from my usual eight-mile morning jog and I am cross.'

'Yeah, I'd be cross if I had to run eight miles every day,' said Freya.

'No,' said Ms Mustang. 'I am cross because somebody has disobeyed my instructions.'

She pointed in the direction of the campfire remains and the sitting logs. There was the special wooden marshmallow box. The padlock was still on it, but there was a large hole in the side. And the box was empty.

Class Red gasped.

Ms Mustang put her arm in the air. In her hand she held . . .

'A Bad Leaf!' said Tamsin.

'Will the person or unicorn who did this please do the right thing and come forward,' said the teacher.

There was a silence. The children all looked at one another. Jake was glaring at Dave. He obviously thought it was him, but he wasn't saying anything – probably because if Dave got the Bad Leaf, then

their whole team wouldn't be able to do the ropes course. But Mira knew it *wasn't* Dave, as she had been with him all night!

'Okay,' said Ms Mustang. 'Did anyone leave their tent last night?'

All eyes turned to Mira and Dave.

'Well . . . us,' said Mira. 'Dave needed to use the toilet bucket.'

'And did you break into the box?' said Ms Mustang in a very serious voice.

'No!' said Mira.

'Dave?' said Ms Mustang.

Dave shook his head furiously.

'He just went to the toilet!' said Mira. 'And anyway, I was with him. I would have seen if

he broke into the box.'

Dave did an indignant fart. Ms Mustang frowned and looked down at the marshmallow box, and then at Dave.

'I believe them!' said Raheem and the others nodded.

'So you were with him the whole time?' said Ms Mustang to Mira.

'Yes, I . . .' And then Mira stopped. She hadn't actually been with Dave the *whole* time. 'Well, no, he went off to use the bucket, but just for a few minutes . . .'

Ms Mustang raised her eyebrows and Jake glared even more. Some of the others were looking a bit unsure now.

Mira's face felt hot. She knew her unicorn and she knew he hadn't touched the marshmallows! But she didn't know who else could have got into the box.

Or did she?

'The shadow creature!' she said, pointing over at their tent.

'The . . . what?' said Ms Mustang.

'You know!' said Mira, looking around Class Red. 'We all saw it, on the wall of the tent! It was this giant terrifying monster and – and it had giant TEETH that it must have used to bite the box open!'

The others looked at each other, unsure whether to laugh.

'Mira, that was just Jake's shadow puppet,' said
Freya kindly.

'No! Jake had his hands down. It was a real
creature, outside the tent! Jake, tell them!'

Everyone turned to Jake, who was looking
confused. Then all eyes turned back to Mira.
Her shoulders drooped. Then there was a
CREEEAAK sound. Dave had his head
inside the empty box, trying to sniff out any
marshmallow remains.

Ms Mustang raised her eyebrows at Mira again. She held out the Bad Leaf. 'I am afraid that Mira's team will be sitting out the activities today,' she said.

Mira took the Bad Leaf and looked down at her feet. She could feel tears in her eyes. It was so unfair!

Ms Mustang told everyone else to get ready for the ropes course. They began to head back to their tents, looking back at Mira with sympathetic expressions. Mira looked at Jake, who was kicking the ground in annoyance, and Raheem, who was unclipping the special safety harness he'd brought from home.

'M–Ms Mustang?' she said. 'I think Raheem and

Jake should be able to go. Dave and I can stay here.'

Ms Mustang's expression softened. 'That is a very kind thing to do for your team, Mira,' she said. 'As you have accepted responsibility, they can go to the ropes course.'

'Cool!' said Jake and he raced off towards his tent.

Raheem and Darcy and Star and Brave came over. 'I believe that you didn't eat the marshmallows, Dave,' said Raheem.

'I was with you until the bit about the shadow creature,' said Darcy, giving her a hug.

'Thanks guys,' said Mira. 'I just know that Dave's telling the truth. And there's no way

he could have made that big hole in the box.'
She sat down on one of the logs with a thump.
'Anyway, you'd better get ready. I don't want
you to miss the ropes course as well.'

Ms Mustang got everyone lined up ready to
go. Wildebeest was going to stay behind at the
campsite to look after Mira and Dave. Jake said it
wasn't fair that they would get to hang out with
Wildebeest.

'He's basically the coolest unicorn ever!' he
said. Mira saw Pegasus' lower lip wobble, as if he
was about to cry.

'Apart from maybe your UBFF?' Mira said,
hoping Jake would get the hint.

'Huh?' Jake said, turning round. 'Sorry, I

didn't hear you. I was too busy getting ready to be awesome on the ropes course!'

Mira stuck her tongue out at him and then quickly stopped when she saw Ms Mustang turn round. The teacher clapped and then the rest of Class Red followed her out of the campsite. Wildebeest gave Ms Mustang an army-style salute. The other children waved at Mira and Dave, but Raheem sat down next to Mira.

'I don't mind sitting it out with you,' Raheem said. 'Brave and I wanted to add to our rock collection and I'd been worrying we wouldn't have time with all the activities.'

'Yeah, me too,' said Darcy, wheeling over

to Mira. 'Well, not the rocks – but I did a ropes course for my birthday, so I'm over it. To be honest, I actually got banned because I kept overtaking people who were slowing me down.'

Mira managed to convince her friends not to miss out on the ropes course. She'd still have Dave to hang out with after all. And they could find some rocks for Raheem. Plus, they would never hear the end of it if Jake got the prize for being the best. Mira was still feeling cross with him for not speaking up about the strange shadow monster thing!

Raheem and Darcy went off to join their classmates. Despite being disappointed about the

Bad Leaf, Mira felt a little glow. Knowing they had been prepared to miss the fun to hang out with her made her feel much better. Her friends were the best!

CHAPTER TEN
I Spy...?

Dave hopped on to the log next to Mira. He nibbled her ear and did an affectionate fart.

'Thanks Dave,' Mira said and she leaned her head against his. She knew this was rubbish for him as well. Everyone thought he'd lied AND he hadn't actually got to eat any of the marshmallows. And Mira did feel a bit sad that she wouldn't be able to find the Golden Marshmallow and share it with everyone. Especially as Rani had seen the Golden Marshmallow near the ropes course! This outdoor adventure holiday wasn't turning out the way she'd hoped at all.

Mira hugged her knees into her chest and watched Wildebeest doing one-hooved press-ups.

Dave started nibbling at her socks.

'Ha ha!' she giggled. 'Okay stop it now, Dave – it tickles!'

But Dave did it again. Soon Mira was laughing so hard she thought she might never stop. And then she fell off the log, still laughing. She looked up at her UBFF, who blinked at her and farted. Dave *always* cheered her up!

And so Mira decided she wasn't just going to sit on a log feeling glum. She was on an amazing adventure holiday with her UBFF. They could find something fun to do right here at the campsite!

'What do you want to do, Dave?' she said. 'We could play hide and seek, or climb a tree . . .'

And that's when Mira had an even BETTER

idea. They could climb a tree and use Rani's

binoculars to search for the Golden Marshmallow!

Mira and Dave ran over to their tent. Mira

grabbed her rucksack and tipped it upside down.

There they were – the

blue binoculars, with

RANI written in big

letters on the side.

They ran back to

the middle of the campsite. Mira looked around

the clearing at the trees, to see which was the

most climbable. She saw one with a big wide

trunk and lots of thick, low-down branches.

'Perfect!' she said.

She pulled herself up on to the lowest branch.

Dave hopped up after her. If they could find the Golden Marshmallow and surprise the others with it when they got back that would *totally* make up for missing out on the ropes course.

Mira climbed to the next branch and then the next. Soon she'd reached the highest branch that was strong enough for climbing. She sat down and held the binoculars up to her eyes. Dave curled up next to her and had a snooze.

It was pretty cool, seeing everything up close. She zoomed in on some birds in their nest feeding their little baby chicks. And she saw a squirrel leaping from branch to branch with an acorn in its mouth. She had to keep

making sure she wasn't getting distracted
and to look for glimpses of gold.

Then from below them she heard a rustling,
scrambling, gnawing sound. Just like they'd
heard outside the tent last night, but fainter and
further away. Mira put the binoculars to her eyes
again and focused. There was something moving

on the path. In fact, something was taking up the whole path.

'Dave!' she hissed. 'Wake up! There's something there! It's some sort of . . . giant . . .' Mira's heart leaped into her throat. '. . . shadow creature!'

Dave squealed and jumped into Mira's lap.

Mira's hands were shaking and so were the binoculars. But she took a deep breath and looked again. 'And I think . . . it . . . it's got LOADS OF HEADS!'

Dave squealed again, louder this time, and buried his head in Mira's T-shirt. Through the binoculars, Mira saw all the monster's heads turn round.

'Oh, no, wait. It's lots of small animals,' she said.

Dave climbed off her and sat down on the branch again.

A few of the animals opened their mouths, revealing big toothy grins.

'They're beavers!' Mira said. 'Wow!'

She watched as the beavers scampered over to the side of the path. Mira followed them with the binoculars. They crowded round a tree trunk and then started to gnaw it. Wow, Mira thought. This was like watching a real-life nature documentary!

The tree creaked and then crashed to the ground. Some of the beavers rolled it along

with their paws towards
the river, while the others
rushed off into the woods.

Mira's heart stopped. They were
heading towards the ropes course, where
the rest of Class Red were!

'Dave! What if the beavers cut down the trees
that the ropes are connected to?' cried Mira.

They had to warn the rest of their class! Mira
and her unicorn quickly scrambled back down
the tree to tell Wildebeest what was going on.

'Wildebeest?' Mira called, looking all around
for Ms Mustang's unicorn. She couldn't see him
anywhere. Perhaps he was doing something
brave and outdoorsy. Or perhaps he was just

really camouflaged. 'Um, so we're just going to go and rescue the others in case the beavers gnaw down the trees while they're up on the ropes course?'

There was no reply.

Mira hung the binoculars around her neck. Then she ran to her tent and looked inside. Raheem's area was incredibly tidy. And there, next to his spare wellies, was a spare climbing harness and some rope. She grabbed them. Dave appeared behind her and grabbed a few bags of emergency crisps. They climbed out of the tent and Mira jumped on to Dave's back.

'Let's go!' she cried.

They galloped off towards the rope course as

fast as Dave's little legs would carry them. It was easy to track the beavers' path as lots of trees and branches had been gnawed and fallen down.

And then, as they trotted along, Mira saw something out of the corner of her eye.

A glimmer of gold.

She tried to look through the binoculars – but it was hard to hold them still (Dave only had little legs and so riding him was very bouncy). But she was sure there was something glittery lying just beyond those bushes . . . Maybe they could quickly go and look? What if the Golden Marshmallow was close by . . .?

But Mira knew she had to make sure that her class was safe.

Mira focused the binoculars again and spotted the beavers. They'd gathered around another tree. Mira pointed the binoculars upwards. Attached to the top of the tree was the far end of a rope bridge.

Dave and Mira sped along the forest path. Mira was keeping her eye on the beavers. One of them was passing something round to the others. Mira squinted into the binoculars.

'They're eating marshmallows!' she yelled. 'The beavers stole them! They must have used their strong teeth to gnaw through the box!'

Now the start of the rope bridge swung above them. Just before it, there was a tightrope with a rope above to hold on to, leading to a platform. Shimmying along the tightrope was

Ms Mustang, followed by Class Red.

Mira heard a loud gnashing sound up ahead. The beavers had finished their stolen snack and were starting to gnaw the tree holding up the other end of the rope bridge!

'STOP! Beavers!' yelled Mira, jumping up and down on Dave's back. 'Beavers ahead! Gnawing down the tree! STOP!'

But the class were too high up to hear her! They were on the platform now, moving towards the rope bridge.

'I need to get up there,' said Mira, slipping into Raheem's harness. She clipped the harness on to the rope and threw the rope up over a branch. 'Grab the end, Dave!'

Dave grabbed the end of the
rope in his mouth.

'Now,' Mira said, 'once
I'm up, you run and try to
make the beavers stop!'

Dave nodded. He pulled on the rope, walking
backwards. It went tight, and then Mira was
being pulled up into the trees.

Ms Mustang and Jake had stepped on to the rope
bridge, followed by Darcy riding Star.

'Wait!' Mira yelled again as she got nearer to them.

This time Ms Mustang did look down. And
when she saw Mira she looked VERY cross.

Mira grabbed on to the platform. Dave let go of his end of the rope and galloped on towards the beavers. Suddenly Mira felt very high up.

Ms Mustang leaned across and helped Mira on to the rope bridge. The teacher's expression was still furious.

'Oh, are you joining in after all?' said Darcy, clipping Mira's harness on to the safety rope.

'Listen!' said Mira, and then she explained all about the beavers . . .

Ms Mustang peered across to the next tree. 'Move back, everyone!' she said.

But as she did, there came a loud

CREEEEEEEEEEEEEAAAAAAAAAAAK

The tree was already falling! And Mira, Darcy, Jake and Ms Mustang were still standing on the rope bridge!

Mira felt the rope bridge falling away beneath them. The four of them shot forward. Now they were zipwiring as the tree ahead of them began to fall to the ground.

'ARRRRRGGGGGGGGGGHH!' screamed Mira, Jake and Ms Mustang.

'THIS IS SO MUCH FUN!' yelled Darcy. 'Hey, are those the beavers you were talking about?'

Mira looked up. The beavers weren't on the ground any more. They were standing straight ahead, one on top of the other, in a furry, very

wobbly, tower. And climbing to the top of the tower . . . was a plump little unicorn.

CHAPTER ELEVEN
Flying Unicorn

'Dave!' cried Mira.

Dave snorted and held his front legs out wide.

'He's going to catch us!' said Mira.

'Er, HOW?' yelled Jake.

But Mira didn't have time to answer – or to think about what Dave might be doing – because right then they zipwired right into the little unicorn.

Mira somersaulted through the air and landed with her legs around Dave's neck. Ms Mustang and Darcy were squished together on his back,

and Jake tumbled through the air and ended
up upside down, clinging to Dave's bum. Mira
held on tight to her UBFF. And now they were
flying through the air!

Ms Mustang and Jake screamed again. Darcy started improvising some dramatic background music.

'I can't believe we're flying a unicorn!' cried Mira.

She saw something up ahead. Something gold and glowing, glimmering through the trees.

'We're not flying, we're FALLING!' yelled Jake from Dave's bum.

They soared through the air, skimming the tops of the trees. The glimmering golden shape got closer and then they started to dip. Jake was right – they WERE falling. Mira put her arms up over her face as they ploughed through the branches. She braced herself for impact . . .

FLUMP!

They landed in something very soft and squishy. And it smelled absolutely delicious.

THE GOLDEN MARSHMALLOW!

Ms Mustang and Jake looking rather dazed. Darcy was looking thrilled. Dave was sitting with the beavers, happily tucking into the Golden Marshmallow.

But there wasn't just one Golden Marshmallow.

There was a whole glowing group of them!

∪∪∪

When everyone had recovered, Ms Mustang and
Jake went back to help the other children and
unicorns, while Mira, Darcy and Dave picked
lots of Golden Marshmallows to bring back
for the campfire. Well, Mira and Darcy picked
them. Dave just carried on eating. The beavers
made a little pile of Golden Marshmallows and
nudged them along the ground towards Mira.

'Thanks, friends!' she said, with a grin. She
told the others how it was the beavers who'd got
into the marshmallow box, not Dave. 'I think
they needed lots of energy for gnawing down
trees,' she said. 'They must be building a dam!'

The beavers all nodded and made chirping
sounds. One of them did a marshmallowy burp.

When the others and their unicorns arrived,
they all helped the beavers to roll their logs
down to the river. Then they all headed back to
the campsite while Darcy explained everything

that had happened. Jake was boasting that he had

travelled down the zipwire at the fastest speed.

'I can't wait to tell Wildebeest about it!' he

said as they reached the campsite.

Mira saw Pegasus's nose droop and he trotted

off in the direction of their tent. She tried to

catch up with Jake, but he had already raced off to look for Wildebeest.

But the campsite was empty. Where *was* Wildebeest?

'Let's get out my special celebratory tea set!' called Darcy, trotting along on Star towards her yurt.

'Hey!' she yelled a few seconds later.

Mira peered through the open yurt door. There was Wildebeest, sitting in Darcy's hot tub with cucumbers on his eyes and headphones on, singing tunelessly.

Jake stood next to Mira and stared, his mouth dropping open in disappointment.

'Well, even the toughest unicorns need time

to chill!' said Mira with a grin.

A cough came from behind them. It was Pegasus. He coughed again, and then he trotted off towards Jake and Mira's tent. He turned back to see if they were following.

Jake ran after him and Mira followed too. The unicorn stopped just behind the tent and proudly presented Jake with . . .

. . . a tent made out of leaves.

Jake stared, open-mouthed. 'That is SO cool, Pegasus!' he said.

The others came over to see what was going on. They all admired the leaf-tent too.

'Yeah, well, my unicorn *is* the cleverest, most awesome unicorn there is!' said Jake with a grin.

Pegasus blushed and looked very pleased.

'That's the weirdest tent I've ever seen,' said Darcy, appearing behind Mira. 'Anyway, Ms Mustang says can we come over and help to start the campfire.'

∪∪∪

The Golden Marshmallows glowed and glittered even more in the evening light. And they were the tastiest, toastiest marshmallows that any of them had ever tasted or toasted!

Flo hoovered up the marshmallow from her toasting fork like a marshmallow vacuum cleaner and swore she would never eat anything except Golden Marshmallows for the rest of her life.

Raheem and Brave waved their glowing marshmallow sticks like sparklers and the glow led them to a couple of nice glittering rocks on the ground for their collection.

Jake said that Pegasus should get the biggest marshmallow for making the tent of leaves. Darcy said it should be given to Mira and Dave, for saving their lives. But while they were arguing, Dave ate it.

Mira took the last marshmallow and wrapped it in a leaf. She took her pen out of her pocket and wrote **RANI** on the leaf in big letters. She couldn't wait to give it to her sister! (And she hoped that it would distract her from the fact that her binoculars had been

broken during the zipwire landing.)

The campfire crackled and sparked in the moonlight, and everyone started to sing songs. Mira grinned happily. She knew that deep in the Wild Woods the beavers were happily building a new dam with the trees they had cut down.

Next to Mira, Dave did a happy burp. Mira gave her UBFF a hug.

'Outdoor adventure holidays are the best,' she whispered in his ear. 'And especially when you're with your UBFF!'

HOW **WILD** ARE YOU?

1. What do you pack on a trip to the woods?
   a. I need nothing but my wits.
   b. Everything on the kit list plus emergency supplies of first aid, emergency rations and emergency socks.
   c. Just the essentials: face mask, hot tub, slippers, bunting, fairy lights, choc ice . . .
   d. Whatever I can stuff in the bag!

2. What's your favourite campfire treat?
   a. Toasted marshmallows.
   b. Toasted marshmallows.
   c. A full cream tea with four types of sandwiches and six types of cakes.
   d. Toasted marshmallows.

3. What are you most scared of in the woods?
   a. NOTHING.
   b. Spiders.
   c. Running out of cream tea.
   d. Dave going hungry.

4. How far would you venture from the camp?
   a. THE EDGE OF THE WOODS AND BEYOND – AS FAR AS THE EYE CAN SEE AND THE MIND CAN IMAGINE.
   b. As far as the teacher says we can go.
   c. I have everything I need in my tent thanks.
   d. As far as the mood takes me!

5. How do you cross a river?
    a. Build a raft from whatever nature provides.
    b. Tie careful knots in rope over barrels to paddle.
    c. IN STYLE!
    d. Propelled by Dave's fart jet.

6. You hear a noise at night in the woods, what do you do?
    a. Investigate.
    b. Hide.
    c. Put on my noise-cancelling headphones.
    d. Have some snacks.

Answers:

Mostly As: you are Jake and Pegasus! Fearless forest friends, you are natural born explorers, and survivors. **Totally wild.**

Mostly Bs: you are Raheem and Brave! You're sensible and don't take risks. **Safely wild.**

Mostly Cs: you are Darcy and Star! No one has ever camped with more style. **Fabulously wild.**

Mostly Ds: you are Mira and Dave! You have the tastiest time in the woods and have accidental amazing adventures. **Chaotically wild.**

Catch up on ALL of Mira and Dave's Adventures at Unicorn School!

THE NAUGHTIEST UNICORN ON A SCHOOL TRIP

PIP BIRD
ILLUSTRATED BY DAVID O'CONNELL

THE NAUGHTIEST UNICORN ON THE BEACH

Fun in the sun!

PIP BIRD
ILLUSTRATED BY DAVID O'CONNELL

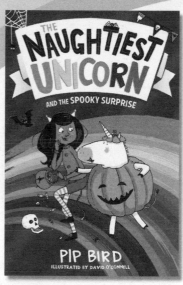

THE NAUGHTIEST UNICORN AND THE SPOOKY SURPRISE

PIP BIRD
ILLUSTRATED BY DAVID O'CONNELL

THE NAUGHTIEST UNICORN IN A WINTER WONDERLAND

PIP BIRD
ILLUSTRATED BY DAVID O'CONNELL

COMING SOON!